THE FLIGHT OF A DOVE

The *Flight* of a DOVE

ALEXANDRA DAY

FARRAR STRAUS GIROUX
NEW YORK

Thank you to Elise Robinson and Margaret Mahoney
for their help.

—A.D.

Copyright © 2004 by Alexandra Day
All rights reserved
Distributed in Canada by Douglas & McIntyre Ltd.
Color separations by Hong Kong Scanner Arts
Printed in the United States of America by Berryville Graphics
Designed by Robbin Gourley and Jay Colvin
First edition, 2004
1 3 5 7 9 10 8 6 4 2

www.fsgkidsbooks.com

Library of Congress Cataloging-in-Publication Data
Day, Alexandra.
    The flight of a dove / Alexandra Day.— 1st ed.
        p. cm.
    Summary: Four-year-old Betsy, an autistic child, begins to
improve after she sees a dove, one of the animals at her
preschool, fly into the air. Based on a true story.
    ISBN 0-374-39952-2
    [1. Autism—Fiction. 2. Animals—Fiction. 3. Birds—Fiction.]
    I. Title.

PZ7.D32915 Fl 2004
[Fic]—dc21

                                                            2002192543

Author's Note

When I first read the account of a little French girl's release from her isolated, apparently autistic state through the flight of a dove in *Why the Wild Things Are*, by Gail F. Melson, it sent a thrill of recognition down my spine. The ability of animals to help children in trouble has been proven to me over and over. My own "Good Dog Carl," a wonderful Rottweiler named Zabala, was a therapy dog, and we worked with children in many hospitals and rehabilitation centers. I saw a child's epileptic seizures stop when she made contact with Zabala. A child who hadn't spoken for months said his first words to the dog. A supposedly paralyzed little hand moved a few inches to touch an inviting muzzle.

I am not a scientist, and although the central facts of the French case are well documented, it occurred many years ago and much of the background is obscure. My retelling of this story must therefore be something of a fable rather than an expert's report.

The powerful and essential truth of this little girl's story, which I hope my version will convey, is the important role that animals can play in the comforting, balancing, and healing of us humans. And I want to share the great joy of that moment when a child begins to heal.

Betsy was a bright, happy baby for the first year or so of her life. Then she began to change. Instead of being interested in exploring the world, she became more and more fearful and easily upset by anything new. Neither her mother nor anyone else around her knew what to do, and by the time she was three and a half, Betsy had withdrawn so completely that she disliked being touched, would eat no solid food, made no sounds except a kind of hissing or clicking, and, if left to herself, would sit for hours swaying slightly with her arms stiff at her sides. Her face would be either blank or twisted into a grimace, her eyes focused on nothing.

At this point, her mother was able to get her into a school which everyone hoped would help her, but Betsy's condition was extreme, and the staff warned her mother that they could make no guarantees.

The first day at Green Meadows School was awful. Betsy sobbed when the head teacher, Mrs. Bouvier, helped her off with her coat.

Then Betsy sat motionless on the floor for two hours without moving. Attempts to comfort her seemed to make things worse. At lunchtime she drank a little milk, but completely rejected the crackers and pieces of fruit.

Tick Tick Tick

The afternoon was not much better. Betsy would not look at any object the teachers brought her. Her only response was sharp little clicks of distress whenever anyone got too near.

Betsy's mother, Jeanne, watched it all with a heavy heart. What, she asked herself for the thousandth time, had made her once-lively daughter change so much?

Mrs. Bouvier put an arm around Jeanne.

"Try not to lose hope," she said. "You believe that Betsy is an extraordinary child. It will take time and patience to help her, but that doesn't mean it can't be done."

Day followed day. Betsy went to school, and she grew to accept this without anxiety and tears, but there was little change in her. After much patience and work, Betsy was persuaded to eat crackers, and would allow the teachers to hand blocks to her.

Her play, however, still consisted of holding them out in front of her, one after another.

Sometimes Betsy would arrange
the blocks in a row or a pile.

Occasionally she made patterns with
her cards, but the patterns were
always the same. Eventually she
let the teacher change the patterns
and suggest new ones, and even
began to experiment with the
cards herself, but only after the
teacher had turned away.

The teachers and Betsy's mother continually tried to interest her in things other than her few favorite objects. What was going on inside her? How could she remain cut off from almost everything? Was she not starved for the affection that all children crave? Why couldn't she respond to the loving hearts reaching out to her?

Mrs. Bouvier's one-year-old daughter cheerfully babbled to her by the hour, but Betsy ignored her unless she tried to get too close. Then she hissed and clicked until someone removed the baby.

Mrs. Bouvier firmly believed that animals could play a valuable role in child development, particularly for a child with special difficulties. So Green Meadows had a number of resident birds and animals. There was a parrot whose name was Captain Flint; two rabbits named Hunch and Bunch; Juniper, a large orange cat; Brownie, a large beagle mixed with something; and a dove whom nobody had gotten around to naming.

These animals were popular with the other children, but Betsy would have nothing to do with any of them.

Brownie was very concerned.
With his generous nature,
he wanted badly to break
through the sadness
he felt in Betsy.

He tried gifts and tricks
to show her how friendly he
was, but all he got
was hissing and
cringing.

Everyone hoped that the springtime would somehow thaw Betsy, too. Perhaps music on the lawn . . . the perfume and beauty of the flowers? But Betsy remained closed in her cold gray world.

Betsy had been at school a year now. Her mother's heart was heavy with discouragement and self-reproach. Had she done wrong to insist on this school? Could she have prevented her daughter's original withdrawal into such a terrible state? Even the teachers were reluctantly coming to the conclusion that, with all their knowledge, skill, and patience, they could not help this child.

Then one day, as the dove was walking near Betsy, another child made a sudden movement and startled the bird into flight.

The flash of the soft white wings rising before her broke through the vacancy of Betsy's stare. For the first time in all these long, discouraging months, Betsy looked and saw the beauty of a living creature.

Her eyes followed its lovely flight. Like spring coming
to a frozen landscape, her rigid face softened and Betsy
smiled.

That was all. The dove alighted and Betsy sat still, but
there was a subtle change in her. Mrs. Bouvier held her
breath and prayed.

The next day Mrs. Bouvier contrived to have the dove near Betsy, and whenever it flew up, Betsy again followed it with her eyes and smiled.

Soon Betsy was imitating the soft sounds of the dove, instead of her old hard noises. She raised her arms in imitation of its wings, and she reached out to touch it.

Finally, one happy
day, when one of the
teachers held the
dove out to her, she
kissed it.

Betsy did not, of course, become a normal child overnight. There were days when she seemed to slip back into her isolation. But slowly, surely, she was changing.

All of the animals now began to attract her attention. She watched Brownie playing with the other children, and when he came wagging his tail, she put out her hand. Brownie was delighted. He took it as a personal triumph when she began petting and kissing him, too.

Betsy was still very wary of people, and Mrs. Bouvier cautiously introduced her into games. Musical games worked best. At first Betsy would not touch the other children, but before long she was willing to hold hands for games like Ring-around-a-Rosy and Skip to My Lou.

Betsy's lack of language still worried everyone. She was now four and a half years old and had never made anything but very primitive noises. She had, however, ceased to hiss and cluck and was attempting to imitate some of the sounds around her. Her love for the dove had led her to imitate its cooing; her friendship with Brownie brought attempts to "talk" his language. She then began to accompany the music of the games with a wordless singsong.

Finally the great day came when Betsy gathered up all of her courage and said her first word . . .

"Mommy!"